phoenix international publications, inc.

Welcome to Zahramay Falls, where twin genies-in-training Shimmer and Shine live with their pets, Tala and Nahal. Look for these landmarks as Shimmer and Shine soar high above:

When Shimmer and Shine are looking for the best bargains in Zahramay Falls, they head to the Azar Bazaar. Can you help the genie sisters browse the market for these treats and trinkets?

this genie bottle

this bottle

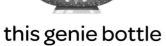
bananas

flying carpet

shoes

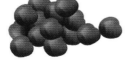
plums

Sun, sand, surf, and...sisters! When the temperature rises, Shimmer and Shine have a magical day at Bela Beach. Stroll along the shore and locate these seaside things:

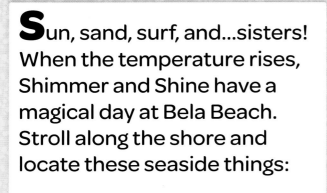

ball

crab

beach chair

sunglasses

this palm tree

bucket

Shimmer and Shine grant three wishes a day to their best friend Leah. Today, Leah has called Shimmer and Shine to help her bake cupcakes. Search for these things in Leah's kitchen:

this bowl

this measuring cup

oven mitt

this spoon

pan

mixer

When Leah's neighbor Zac comes over to put on a magic show, Leah's secret genies need to do a little magic of their own and disappear! Can you find Shimmer and Shine and these other magical things from Zac's act?

hat

crystal ball

Shimmer

rings

wand

Shine

Shimmer and Shine are in training, so sometimes they grant Leah's wishes in ways she didn't exactly mean. Leah wished for a tree house, but the genies turned her house into a tree! Find some critters lurking in this homey habitat:

swan

chicken

reindeer

elephant

cow

crab

After a divine day together, Shimmer, Shine, and Leah turn on their favorite music and have a genie-rific dance party! Help them find all these colorful dresses to add some sparkle to their step:

Back in Zahramay Falls, Shimmer, Shine, Tala, and Nahal play hide-and-seek before snuggling on the sofa. Boom Zahramay—let's play! Look around the twins' living room and find what else is hiding:

book

teacup

Nahal

this lamp

Tala

this plant

Flying carpets aren't the only thing at home in the Zahramay Falls sky. Swoosh back and find these sky-high items:

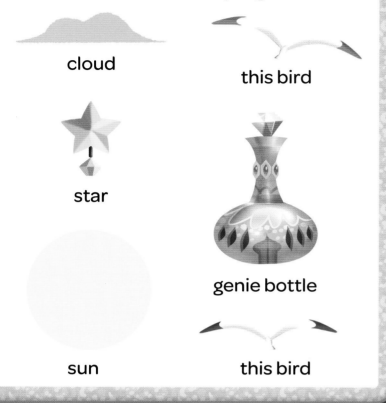

cloud

this bird

star

genie bottle

sun

this bird

Zip back to the market and help Shimmer and Shine find all the things on their list:

pillows

bird cage

elephant

pineapple

this jewel

basket

Splash back to Bela Beach and look for more seaside items. Don't forget your sunscreen!

this shell

this shovel

treasure map

this shell

fish

sand castle

Shimmer and Shine think cupcakes are the yummiest! See if you can find these sweet treats in Leah's kitchen:

Zac's trick didn't go quite right. It happens. It happens a lot. He wanted to pull a rabbit out of his hat, but he got more than he bargained for! Can you find these bouncing bunnies?

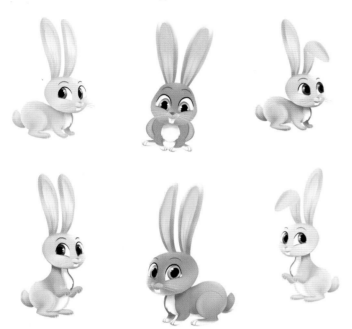

Shimmer and Shine have brought the outside in! Swing back to Leah's living room and find these blooming flowers:

Look around Leah's room for these glittery dance-party costume accessories:

this bangle

this tiara

these necklaces

these earrings

this necklace

this bracelet

Shimmer and Shine are ready to get cozy! Can you find these comfy things?

cuddly horse

this pillow

this blanket

this pillow

teddy bear

these slippers